Dear Parents and Educators,

Welcome to Penguin Young Readers! As parents and educators, you know that each child develops at his or her own pace—in terms of speech, critical thinking, and, of course, reading. Penguin Young Readers recognizes this fact. As a result, each Penguin Young Readers book is assigned a traditional easy-to-read level (1–4) as well as a Guided Reading Level (A–P). Both of these systems will help you choose the right book for your child. Please refer to the back of each book for specific leveling information. Penguin Young Readers features esteemed authors and illustrators, stories about favorite characters, fascinating nonfiction, and more!

Kate & Mim-Mim: Tack and the Beanstalk

LEVEL 2

GUIDED READING LEVEL **I**

This book is perfect for a **Progressing Reader** who:
• can figure out unknown words by using picture and context clues;
• can recognize beginning, middle, and ending sounds;
• can make and confirm predictions about what will happen in the text; and
• can distinguish between fiction and nonfiction.

Here are some **activities** you can do during and after reading this book:
• Make Connections: What would you do if a giant beanstalk grew in your backyard? What do you think you might find at the top?
• Compare/Contrast: This story is a version of a classic fairy tale. Which parts of this story are the same as the original? Which parts are different?

Remember, sharing the love of reading with a child is the best gift you can give!

—Sarah Fabiny, Editorial Director
   Penguin Young Readers program

*Penguin Young Readers are leveled by independent reviewers applying the standards developed by Irene Fountas and Gay Su Pinnell in *Matching Books to Readers: Using Leveled Books in Guided Reading*, Heinemann, 1999.

PENGUIN YOUNG READERS
An Imprint of Penguin Random House LLC

© 2016 KMM Productions Inc. a Nerd Corps company. Licensed by FremantleMedia Kids & Family
Entertainment. Based on the episode "Tack and the Beanstalk" written by Scott and Julie Stewart.
All rights reserved. Published in 2017 by Penguin Young Readers, an imprint of
Penguin Random House LLC, 345 Hudson Street, New York, New York 10014.
Manufactured in China.

ISBN 9780515159110   10 9 8 7 6 5 4 3 2 1

PENGUIN YOUNG READERS

LEVEL 2

PROGRESSING READER

Tack and the Beanstalk

by Lana Jacobs

Penguin Young Readers
An Imprint of Penguin Random House

Kate is happy.

The rain has stopped.

It is time to check on the garden.

"Look at my beanstalk!"

says Kate.

"That's one tall beanstalk,"

says Kate's mom.

"Oh no!

It's so tall that it can't stand up,"

says Kate, worried.

"We can fix that,"

says Kate's mom.

"With a little help, your beanstalk

might grow as tall as the clouds!"

she says.

Kate is so excited.

She twirls Mim-Mim around.

Now they are in Mimiloo!

All of Kate's friends are here.

They look busy.

"What are you doing?" asks Kate.

"You're just in time!"

says Gobble.

"You can help us plant these,"

he says.

Mim-Mim hopes they are
planting carrots.
But they are planting
Boom Beans.

Boom Beans grow superfast.

"As soon as they touch the

ground, they go *boom*!" says Lily.

"Let's see who can grow the biggest Boom Bean beanstalk!" suggests Kate.

The five friends get their

Boom Beans ready.

Boom!

There are five beanstalks now!

But wait!

Here comes Tack with his

Boom Bean.

It's enormous!

"I used my Larger Barger to turn a tiny seed into a big one!" Tack boasts.

"A seed that big could really go . . . ," warns Gobble.

"Boom!" shouts Boomer.

The ground shakes.

Boom!

The beanstalk races up
to the sky.

Oh no!

Lily is on top of that beanstalk!

"We'll get Lily down from there,"

Kate tells everyone.

Boomer has an idea.

"Climb the beanstalk!" he shouts.

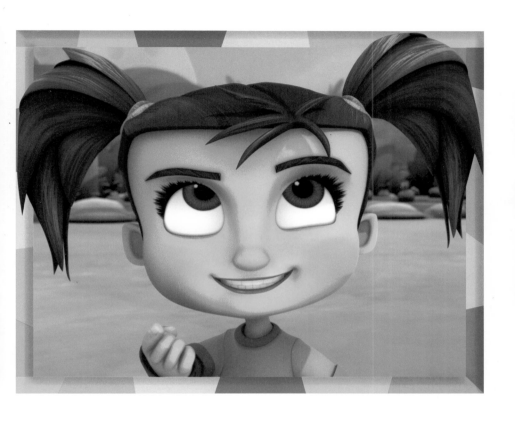

"Come on, everyone!" yells Kate.

"Climb the beanstalk!"

The beanstalk soars straight
through the clouds.
"The tallest beanstalk ever,"
says Mim-Mim.

The friends climb up the beanstalk as fast as they can.

At the top, the friends see a trail
of Boom Bean seeds.

They hope it will lead them
to Lily.

They see a giant castle in
the distance.

What if a giant lives there?

The friends go check it out.

They were right.

A giant does live in the castle!

Mim-Mim is scared.

Wait!

There's Lily!

She is with the giant.

There is no need to worry.

"He's my new friend," says Lily.

"Why does he keep growling

at us?" asks Tack.

It's not a growl—it's his tummy!

The giant is just hungry.

Kate has an idea.

She knows where to find food

big enough for a giant.

"Follow me, everyone!"

she shouts.

The friends give the giant all
of their giant Boom Beans.

The giant is happy now.

So are Kate and all of

her friends!